How the Elephant Got Its Trunk

A Retelling of the
Rudyard Kipling Tale by

Jean Richards

Illustrated by

Norman Gorbaty

Henry Holt and Company · New York

Henry Holt and Company, LLC
Publishers since 1866
115 West 18th Street
New York, New York 10011
www.henryholt.com

Library of Congress Cataloging-in-Publication Data
Richards, Jean.
How the elephant got its trunk : a retelling of the Rudyard Kipling tale /
by Jean Richards; illustrated by Norman Gorbaty.
Summary: Because of her curiosity about what the crocodile has for
dinner, a little elephant and all elephants thereafter have long trunks.
[1. Elephants—Fiction.] I. Kipling, Rudyard, 1865–1936.
II. Gorbaty, Norman, ill. III. Title.
PZ7.R3848 Ho 2003   [E]—dc21   2002007216

ISBN 0-8050-6699-3 / First Edition—2003
The artist used printing ink, rollers, and stencils on paper
to create the illustrations for this book.
Designed by Martha Rago
Printed in Hong Kong
10 9 8 7 6 5 4 3 2 1

To my friend Bernice Chardiet, who started it all
—J. R.

To Joy (my old beauty)—we have seen
the elephant, and it is grand
—N. G.

nce upon a time, in the days before elephants had trunks, when they had only bumps for noses, there lived a little elephant who was very curious. She always asked lots and lots of questions, and since she was very polite she always said, "Excuse me, please," before asking.

There was one thing the little elephant really wanted to know: What does the crocodile eat for dinner? She had already asked her mother, her father, her sister, and her brother, but they would not tell her.

So the little elephant decided to pay a visit to the tall giraffe, who was eating some leaves growing at the top of a tree.

"Giraffe!" she called up to him. "Giraffe!"

"Oh, it's you," sniffed Giraffe, between mouthfuls of leaves. "What is it this time?"

"Excuse me, please," said the elephant as politely as she could. "Can you tell me what the crocodile eats for dinner?"

"You don't want to know!" said Giraffe gruffly, and he moved on to the next tree.

But the little elephant just had to know, so she went to ask the hippopotamus, who was bathing in the lake.

"Hippopotamus!" she called.

"Yes, Little Elephant, what can I do for you?" Hippopotamus said kindly as she swam toward the shore.

"Excuse me, please, but could you tell me what the crocodile eats for dinner?"

Hippopotamus gasped and swallowed some lake water. "Never, never ask that question," she sputtered, and she slipped under the water.

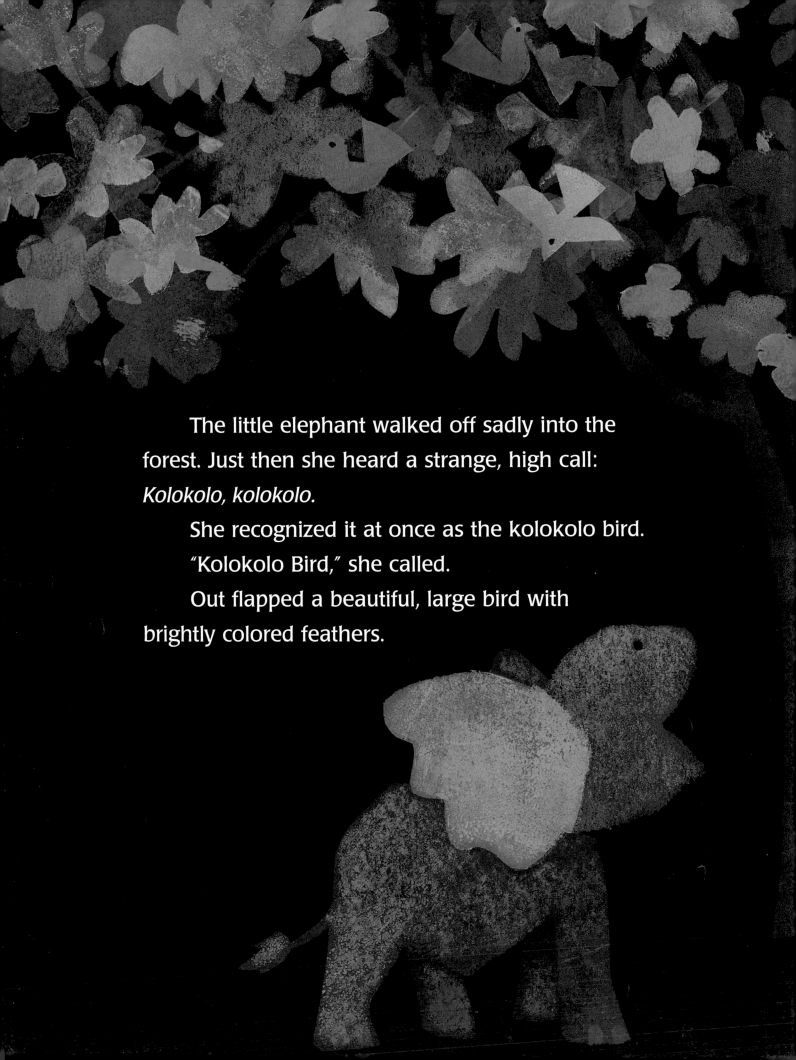

The little elephant walked off sadly into the forest. Just then she heard a strange, high call: *Kolokolo, kolokolo.*

She recognized it at once as the kolokolo bird.

"Kolokolo Bird," she called.

Out flapped a beautiful, large bird with brightly colored feathers.

"P-l-e-a-s-e tell me, I just have to know. What does the crocodile eat for dinner?"

"Go to the banks of the great, gray-green, greasy Limpopo River, where the crocodile lives, and find out for yourself," replied the kolokolo bird.

"The Limpopo?" asked the little elephant, just to make sure.

"Yes, the Limpopo," squawked the kolokolo bird, and it flew off into the trees.

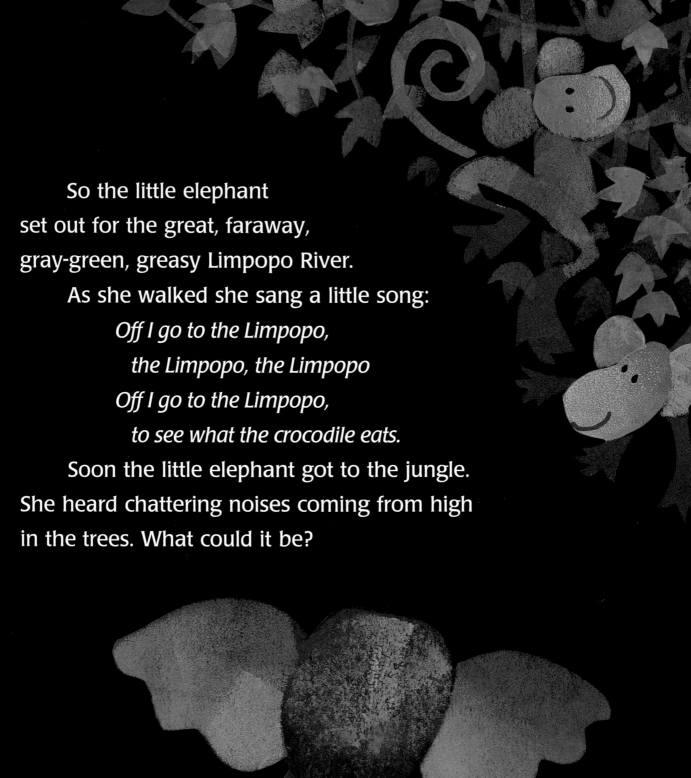

So the little elephant
set out for the great, faraway,
gray-green, greasy Limpopo River.
As she walked she sang a little song:
Off I go to the Limpopo,
the Limpopo, the Limpopo
Off I go to the Limpopo,
to see what the crocodile eats.
Soon the little elephant got to the jungle.
She heard chattering noises coming from high
in the trees. What could it be?

It was a whole family of monkeys swinging from the trees.

"Hi, Little Elephant," they called. "Do you want to play with us?"

"Not now, thank you," she said. "I have no time."

The monkeys waved down at her. The little elephant wanted very much to wave back, but she had nothing to wave with, so she just smiled up at them and continued on her way.

The little elephant came to a clearing and stopped in her tracks. Something was moving in the bushes right next to her. Then she heard an awful roar. What could it be?

Out stepped a huge lion.

As soon as the little elephant saw the lion, she knew he was a friendly one because this lion was smiling and waving at her with his long, swishy tail.

Again, the little elephant wished she could wave back, but she had nothing to wave with, so she just smiled and kept on walking, deeper and deeper into the jungle.

Finally the little elephant came to the banks of the great, gray-green, greasy river called the Limpopo. She sat down to rest.

Then she saw two eyes peering out of the muddy water and a lo-o-o-o-ng snout. What could it be?

It was a huge crocodile. At last the little elephant could get the answer to her question.

"Excuse me, please," she said, as politely as she could. "Can you tell me what you eat for dinner?"

The crocodile looked up at her and winked one eye. "I can't hear you too well," croaked the crocodile. "Come a little closer."

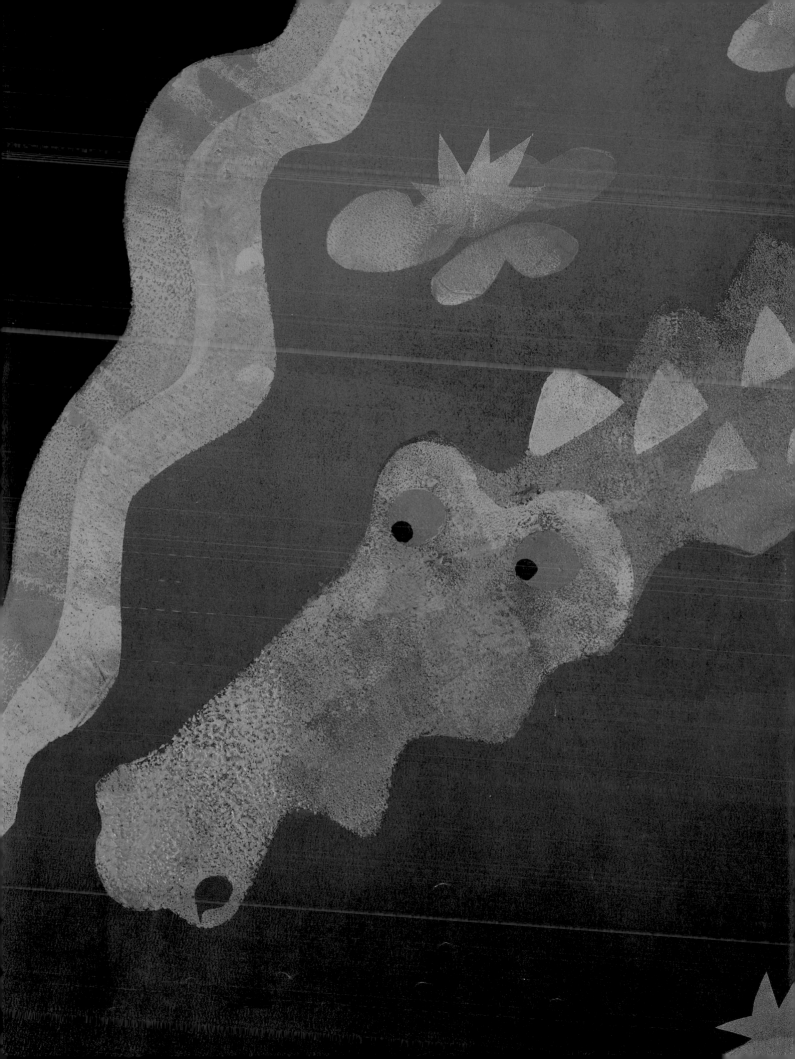

The little elephant kneeled down on the riverbank so she could get very close, and asked again, a bit louder: "Excuse me, please. What do you eat for dinner?"

"If you come even closer," whispered the crocodile, "I'll tell you."

The little elephant got very, very close. Suddenly the crocodile grabbed her little bump of a nose and growled through its teeth, "I eat LITTLE ELEPHANTS for dinner!"

"Oh help!" cried the little elephant. She sat back on her hind legs and began to pull. She pulled as hard as she could, but the crocodile would not let go.

"Whew! That was close!" said the little elephant, and she sat down to catch her breath. "Wait a minute. What's this strange, long, thing where my little bump of a nose used to be?"

At first the little elephant didn't like her new trunk at all. But soon she discovered that she could do all sorts of wonderful things with it.

When a mosquito landed on her back, she could swat at it with her trunk!

When she saw a bunch of ripe yellow bananas hanging high in a tree, she could pick them with her trunk and put them right into her mouth.

When she felt hot and sticky, she could *schloop* up some nice, cool mud, put it on her head, and let it trickle down behind her ears. If she wanted to wash it off, she could give herself a shower.

The little elephant was so excited that she decided to run back home to show all the other elephants her new trunk.

On her way out of the jungle she passed the friendly lion. Now the little elephant had a trunk to wave with, so when the lion waved at her, she proudly waved back at him.

Then she passed the monkey
family. They were eating their dinner.
"Would you like to join us?"
they called.

"I can't," said the little elephant.
"I'm in a rush, but thanks anyway." And
she waved her trunk at them too.

When the little elephant was almost home, she lifted her trunk high in the air and the most amazing sound came out. She found she could also use her trunk as a trumpet: *Ta-da, ta-da!*

When the other elephants heard the trumpet sound, they ran out to see what it was. Imagine their surprise when they saw it was their own little elephant with a beautiful new trunk!

"You look wonderful," they said to her. "Where did you get your new nose?"

"I got it from the crocodile in the Limpopo River," she answered proudly.

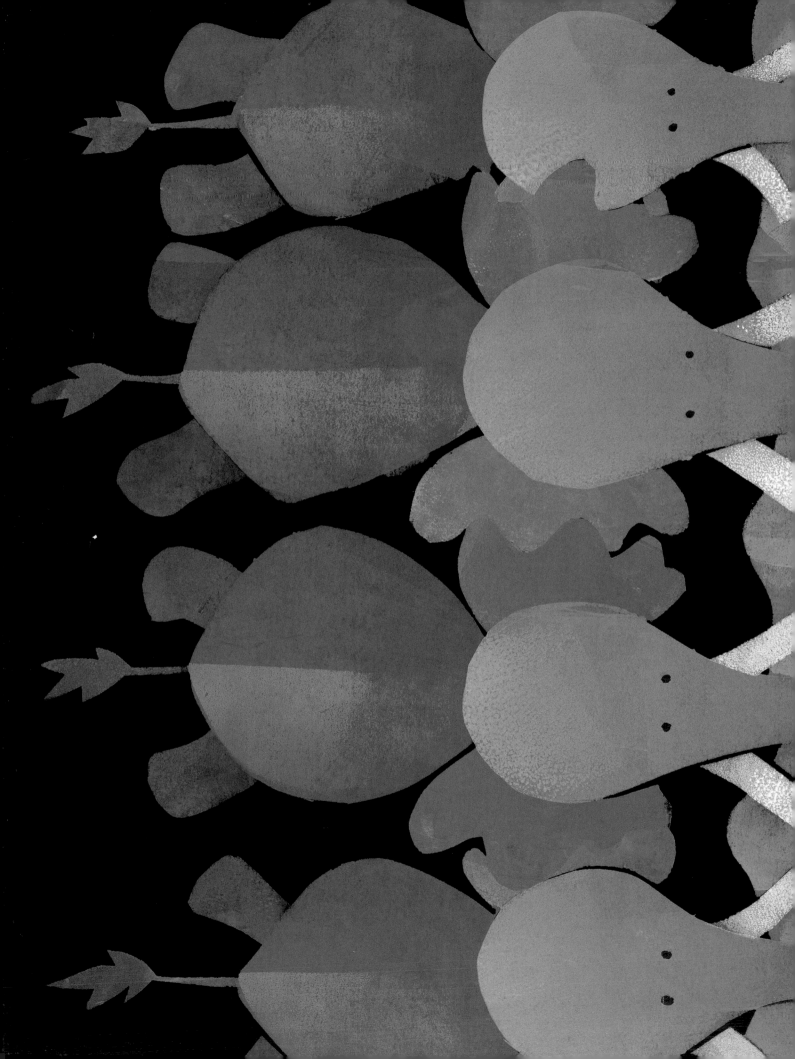

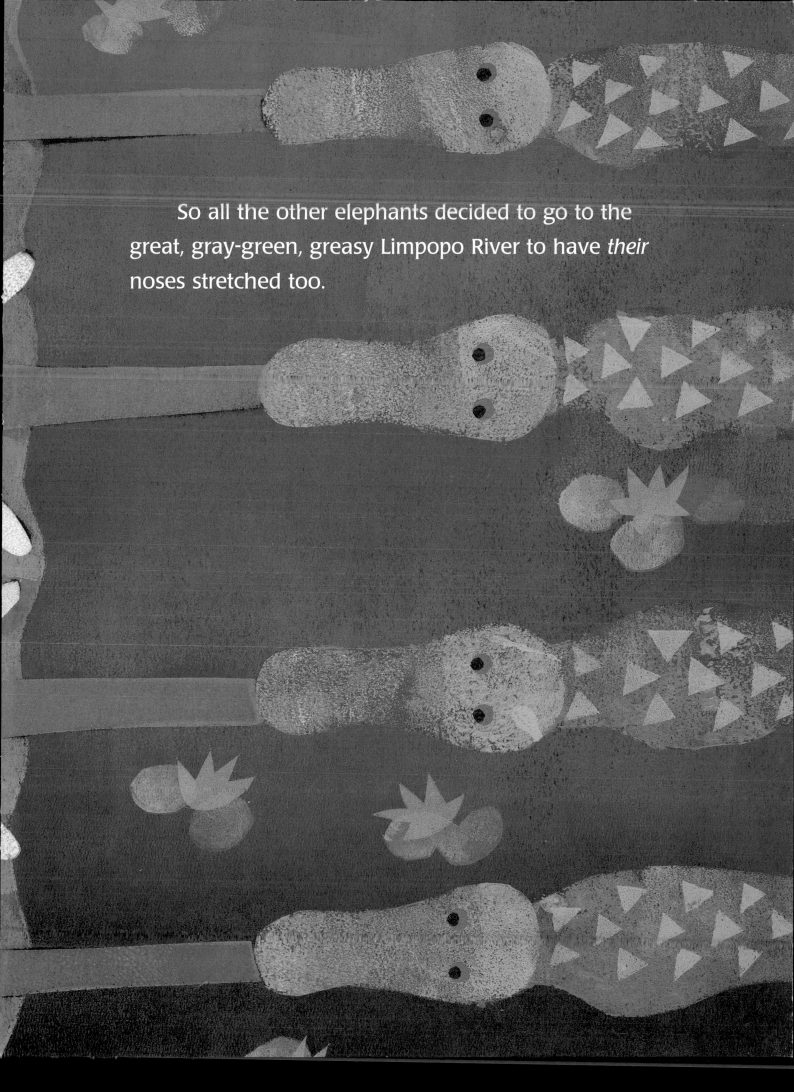

So all the other elephants decided to go to the great, gray-green, greasy Limpopo River to have *their* noses stretched too.

And that is why elephants have trunks today.
At least that is the story.
Do you believe it?